THERE WAS AN OLD LADY WHO SWALLOWED A CACTUS!

by Lucille Colandro

Illustrated by Jared Lee

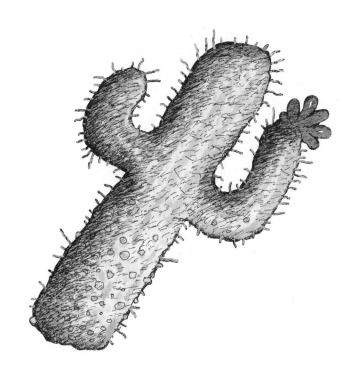

Cartwheel Books

an imprint of Scholastic Inc.

For Martha and Sally, a true oasis of friendship.
– L.C.

In memory of our beloved Skipper, who was the inspiration
for the little black dog who appears in The Old Lady books.
– J.L. and P.J.L.

ISBN 978-1-338-72669-5
10 9 8 7 6 5 4 3 2   21 22 23 24 25
Printed in the U.S.A.   40
First printing, January 2021

There was an old lady who swallowed a cactus.
I don't know why she swallowed a cactus.
But it took lots of practice.

There was an old lady who swallowed some sand.
From out of her hand she swallowed that sand.

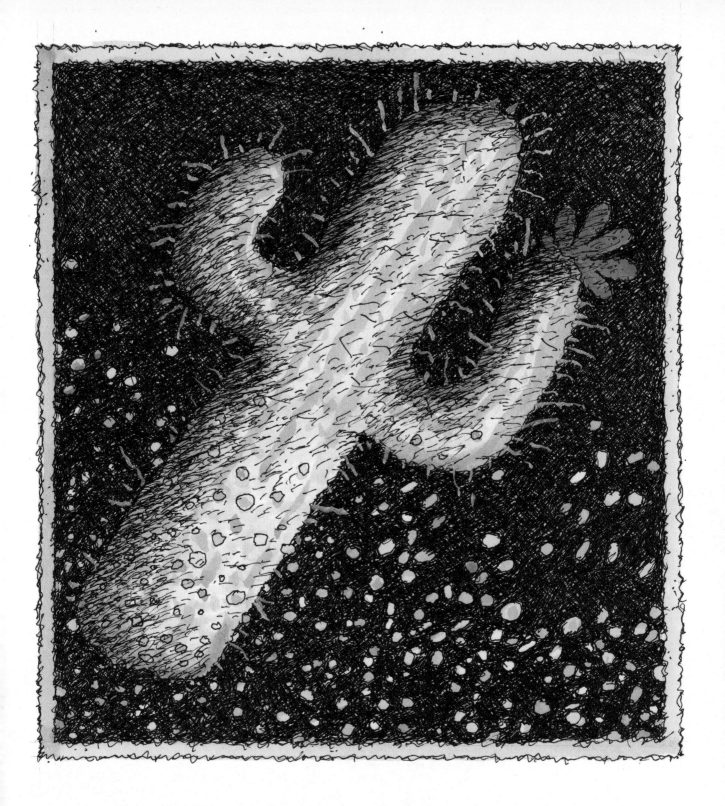

She swallowed the sand to plant the cactus.
I don't know why she swallowed a cactus.
But it took lots of practice.

There was an old lady who swallowed a snake.
What a mistake to swallow a snake.

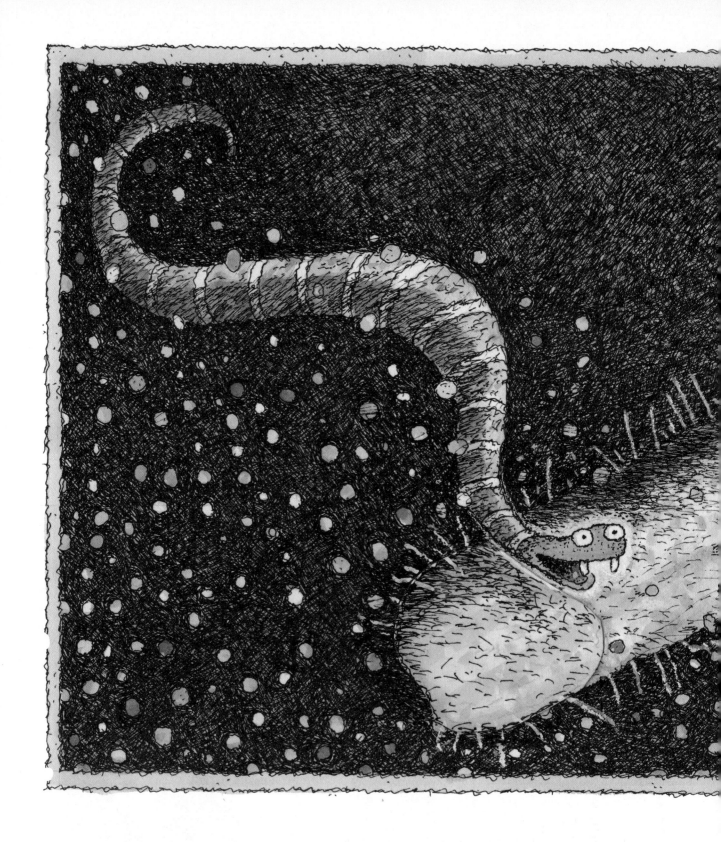

She swallowed the snake to hide in the sand.
She swallowed the sand to plant the cactus.

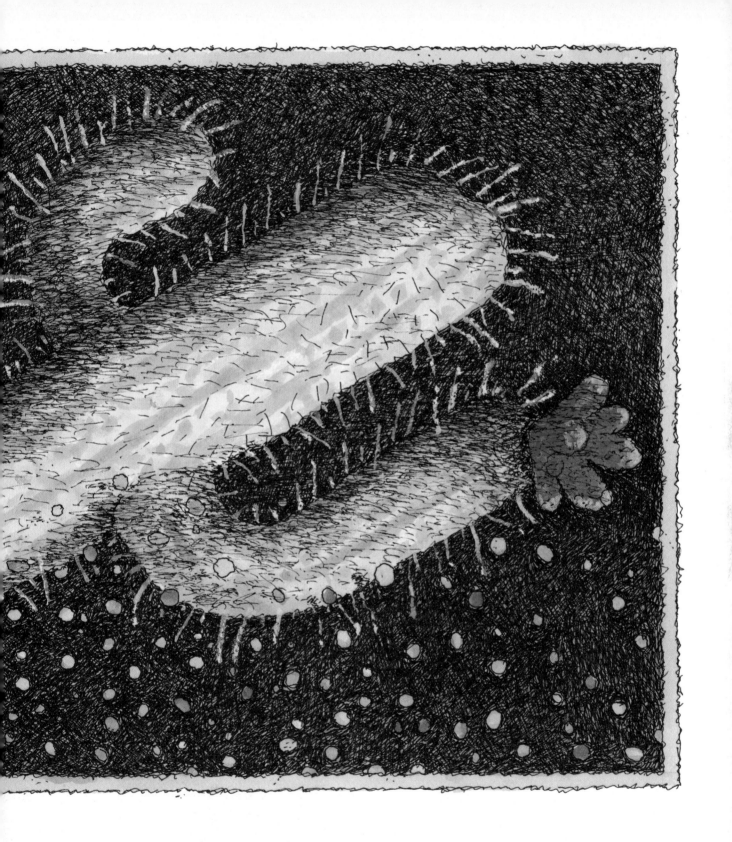

I don't know why she swallowed a cactus.
But it took lots of practice.

There was an old lady who swallowed a coyote.
She felt a bit floaty when she swallowed the coyote.

She swallowed the coyote to track the snake.
She swallowed the snake to hide in the sand.
She swallowed the sand to plant the cactus.

I don't know why she swallowed a cactus.
But it took lots of practice.

There was an old lady who swallowed suntan lotion.
It caused a commotion when she swallowed the lotion.

She swallowed the lotion to cover the coyote.

She swallowed the coyote to track the snake.
She swallowed the snake to hide in the sand.
She swallowed the sand to plant the cactus.

I don't know why she swallowed a cactus.
But it took lots of practice.

There was an old lady who swallowed a canteen.
Everyone had seen her swallow the canteen.

She swallowed the canteen to rinse off the lotion.

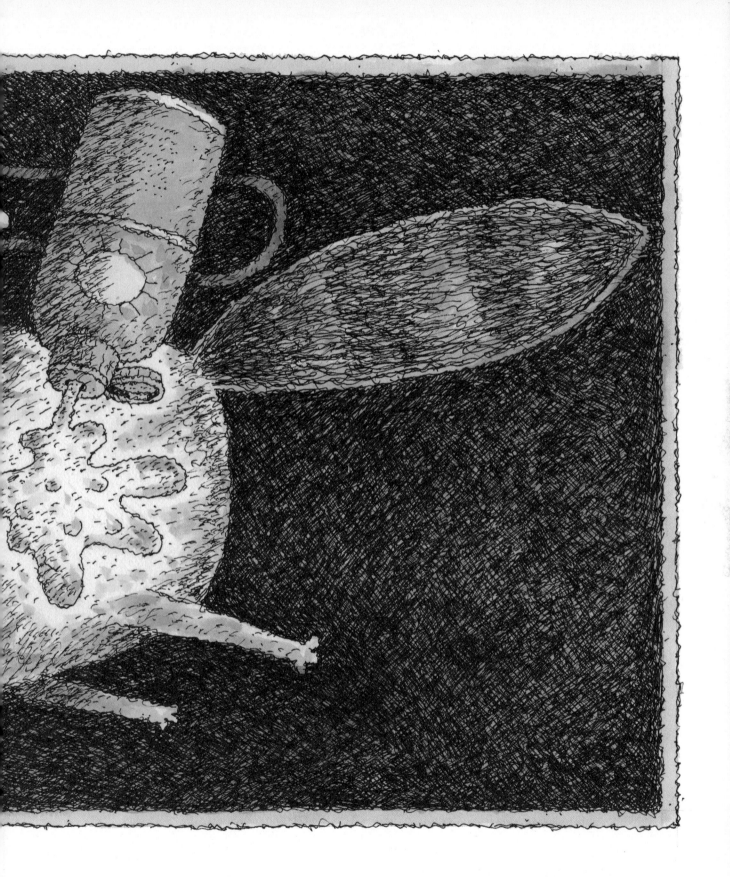

She swallowed the lotion to cover the coyote.

She swallowed the coyote to track the snake.

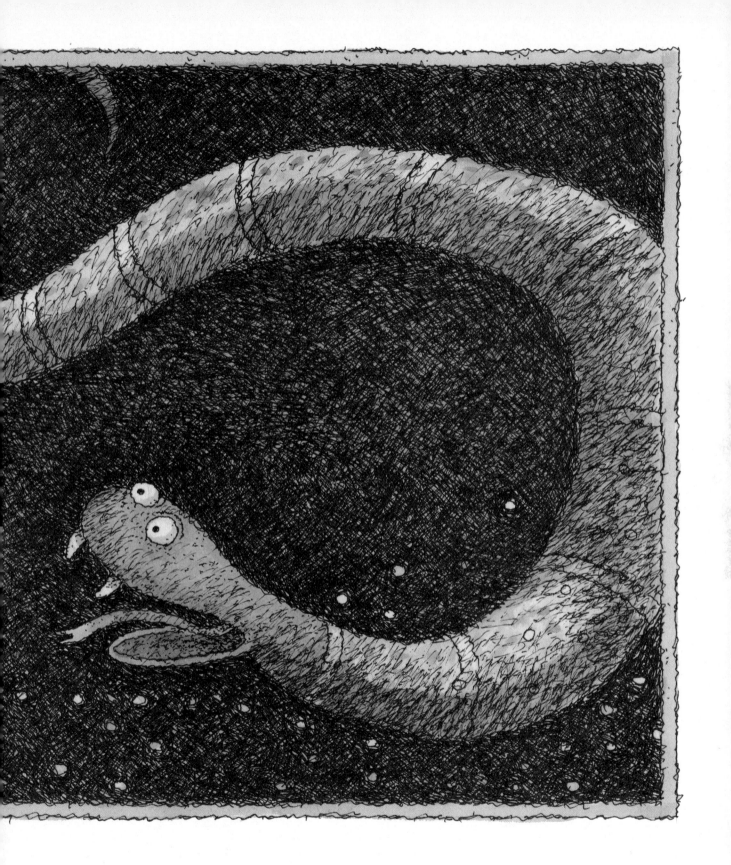

She swallowed the snake to hide in the sand.

She swallowed the sand to plant the cactus.

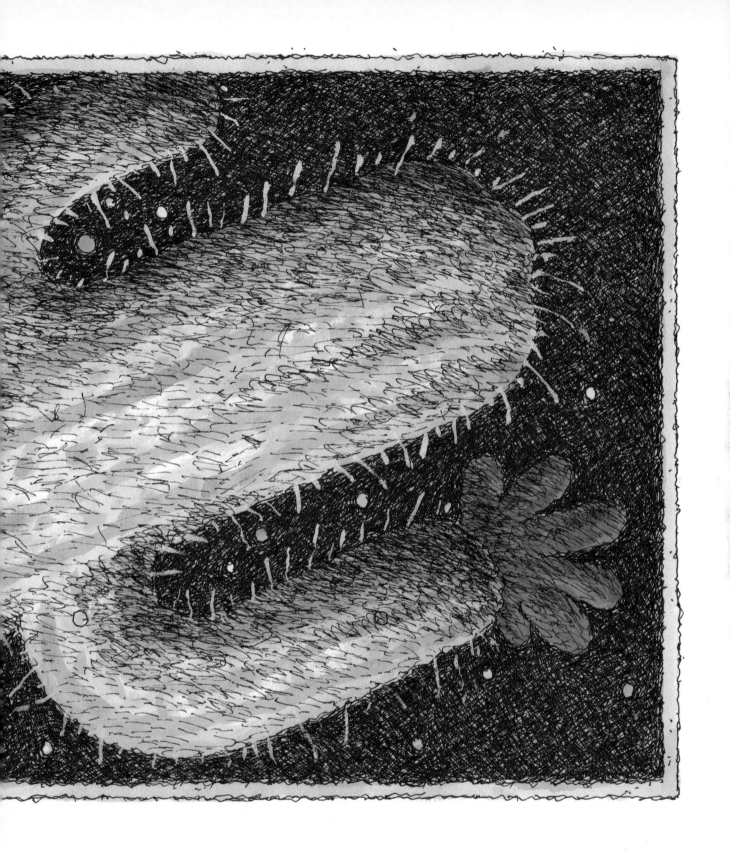

I don't know why she swallowed a cactus.
But it took lots of practice.

There was an old lady who swallowed a parasol.

It was the last of her haul, swallowing a parasol.

The scorching hot sun beating down was the basis . . .

for her to create a perfect desert oasis!